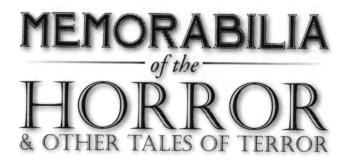

MEMORABILIA
of the
HORROR
& OTHER TALES OF TERROR

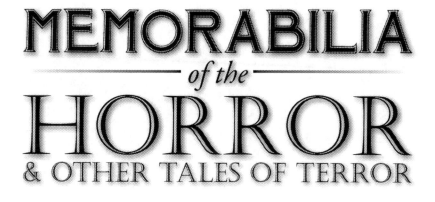

MEMORABILIA
of the
HORROR
& OTHER TALES OF TERROR

Mohammad S. Alwahedi

PARTRIDGE
A Penguin Random House Company

To order additional copies of this book, contact
Toll Free 800 101 2657 (Singapore)
Toll Free 1 800 81 7340 (Malaysia)
orders.singapore@partridgepublishing.com

www.partridgepublishing.com/singapore

Contents

Part II: The Horror in Eynesbury

PART III: The Drawing of the Three

For my grandfather, he who knew ...

Sic parvis magna.
Great things have small beginnings.

Acknowledgements

This work would not have been possible without the contributions made by many people listed below. If, for any reason, someone who means a lot to me does not find his name in this book, then judge me not, for I have a rusty mind and meant no offence at all. I will be sure to list you in my future titles (wink).

To start, I am obliged to thank my family. I express thanks not to my parents, but to my mother and father, each on their own, for giving me this valuable opportunity to achieve my potential. My father has been dutifully vigilant as to the progress made throughout the writing of this book, or 'booklet', as may be nearer to the mark. Thanks to my brother, Sultan and also to Uncle Tariq for frequently inquiring about the developments made. I find myself better in penning down thoughts rather than uttering them.

Thanks are also due to one of my aunts. I have omitted her name for reasons I will keep to myself, but she knows who she is. I express also the warmest of thanks to my uncles and aunts, as numerous as they are.

Moreover, my life would have been as dreary as Poe's if not for my friends. You stood beside me, drawing a smile on my lips whilst I wrote on death and the macabre. So thank you, Salem and Omar. You rock! I also thank Rashed Al-Hammadi, the one and only, for being of assistance.

9

I must thank all of my teachers, be they math teachers or Arabic teachers. However, I owe thanks to a specific few who contributed, whether directly or indirectly, to this book: Mr. Ahmed Balbolia, Mr. Mohammad Al-Najar, Mr. Mohammad Al Trabulsi (who remains as controversial as ever), Mr. Adel Hamana, Mr. Tariq Bahi, and Mr. Adel Chouchan.

As to the ASAD, I must thank four special teachers who influenced me greatly: Mr. Mahmoud Dabet, Ms. Maissa Wahby, and Mrs. Sara Al-Shami, all of whom were great sources of inspiration. I am also very grateful to Mr. Charles Elkins, who aided me in proofreading. He discovered terrible mistakes. Thank you, Mr. Charles!

Thanks go out to my editors at Partridge Publishing, Jade Bailey and Sydney Felicio, for being patient with the development of the manuscript from A to Z. I have been lax and lethargic as of late, and writing the book had become something of a time-consuming burden.

And if inanimate objects could be praised, then I would like to finally thank my closest family, dearest friends, and best teachers: books. Without books my development would have been solely limited to school.

So thank you all. May the sun illuminate your paths as you have lit mine.

At the Crossroads

One can delve into nearly innumerable vistas of hallucination and despair by taking the wrong turn at an intersection. Few can calculate the possibilities. I am one of those few. Indeed, I now wonder whether the strange occurrence on the seventeenth of January was merely an illusion of the mind or a hint that bespoke of horrors we humans are ignorant to.

Being, since my childhood, a man with a natural distaste toward social activities, and yet who admired nature in its quietest, I adopted a habit of having a nocturnal stroll through the suburban streets of Cambridge. My strolls usually began in the middle of the night, when only a few stragglers walked the streets. I usually began from my house, passed by Orchard Park, and then headed to the abandoned railroad tracks, where the streetlamps were devoured by a tangled stretch of trees. In the darkness, a man could scarcely see the outlines of his hands.

On the seventeenth of that month, I began my stroll. The gibbous moon above gave everything a subtle iridescence. I walked slowly, humming to myself peacefully, when I came upon the railroad tracks. As I had memorized the path, I kept walking forward into the dark. Then I stopped. I saw a small, even darker road, which I had never remembered seeing before. And so, propelled on by the sort of curiosity that wrecks the life of a youth, I turned onto the small avenue. For this I paid a price greater than Orpheus, he who looked over his shoulder.

I crawled onward slowly; not a thing stirred. Then I saw it. From a window of a dilapidated house nearby hung a corpse with a rough-spun sack on its head; congealed blood clung to the sack. Just a flicker and everything returned to pitch darkness.

I uttered the most girlish squeak that my male organs could muster, and yet instead of succumbing to fear and retreating from whence I came, I found myself irresistibly drawn toward that particular house. I advanced to the porch and saw that the house's number was 1/3, in the ancient style that English houses were once numbered. I pushed the door, which creaked open, and turned on my phone's torch.

I felt, rather than saw, a body creep beside me. Turning the torch on it, I saw a stark-naked humanoid being—for it was certainly no man—with hunched shoulders and a reddish-purple body. Being no more than eighty centimetres in length, it walked on its hands and feet, ignoring my presence completely.

I froze in place as another of these beings crawled past the open door. Instead of going upstairs, as his kin did, he went to the kitchen. I followed him with a strange spark of fascination that fed my dark fantasies. The kitchen was as dark as darkness can be. I turned around, looking for that hideous beast, yet saw nothing. Suddenly, I saw the same flicker as before, but this time, I saw a woman— where I swear in God's name thrice that there was nothing of the sort before—with her internal organs spilled on the ground, and the latter beast hunched over her entrails, slowly devouring them. The flicker dissipated.

In a moment, my former humanity returned to me, and as I grasped the meaning of all these things, I fled as fast as I could.

Yet, a sort of delirium blinded my senses, and I found myself falling unconscious, as sky and land both became one.

The following day, I woke up to find myself in Trinity Hospital. A nurse confessed to me that a passerby saw me sprawled on the railway in a deep coma the previous morning. As to house 1/3, I made many inquiries into it, and a retired police officer told me that about fifty years ago, two deformed children with malfunctioned brains butchered their parents; one killed the mother, whilst the other hanged his father by means unknown. He added that house 1/3 was destroyed years ago … years and years ago.

A Xypholian Study

So it is that we humans will always remain ignorant to the world we live in. Even great leaps in science are nothing when compared to what is yet to be discovered. Indeed, I, Malcolm Henderson, by a path I hope no one will follow, learned a horror my fragile soul cannot bear. Yet fear of speculation drives me from telling the public my grotesque discovery. Here are my final words, as I believe that some people with considerable imagination may actually absorb what I am about to write. Some might resolve to know why I don't remove the illogical parts. I am afraid that nothing will be left of the story if I did so.

I have spent my life travelling across the world; as an established archaeologist and palaeontologist, it was obligatory for me to visit ancient sites of great splendour and to give lectures to the younger generations. I—who went to the Antarctic and confronted the hoarfrost and rime of that harsh land and who endured the scorching sun of the Arabian Desert—fell to my knees at this discovery. Fate has a sick sense of humour, I suppose, for the greatest discovery that man ever made (I am sure) was right next door! Yet that accursed discovery exacted a great toll on me, and from it I was taught that there are things our race was never meant to learn. I owe the reader a short introduction before laying the discovery forth.

I believe a sane person owns a stable, safe home, where he or she can rest after a wearying day. This luxury, however, has eluded me, as my career necessitated my constant departure. Still, I rented a small apartment to house my bachelor needs at Edgware Road, London, where I rested during the short breaks between my travels. There I had the honour (you'll know why later) to meet a demon from the very depths of hell. As it happened, he lived right next door.

His name was Wilhelm Derby, or so he claimed. He had an aquiline nose, fair hair, and a short-clipped moustache. His demeanour was that of a gentleman, as was his soft, genteel voice. We usually met in the coffee shop downstairs, where we'd take an isolated table and sit together, sipping quietly. I usually dominated the conversation, and thus our talks drifted mostly to matters in *significantia* to my career. Derby presented profound knowledge of many topics, especially the legend of Atlantis. His cool attitude changed into an uncomfortable one as he spoke of it, but he still talked pedagogically. Another strange thing was the palpable pride with which he replied when the topics of Memphis and Babel were discussed. It was as if he had something to do with them.

Mr. Derby looked immaculate to my eyes. However, his skin had a sickly, vaguely gray hue, and several skin lesions adorned his arms, which he claimed were a result of leprosy. He also had a pungent, piquant scent, which had a capsaicin-like effect on me, and thus made me keep my distance when engaged in conversation with him. When uttering the letter *r*, he pronounced it like a German: in a guttural, throaty voice that gave him an artificial edge. All in all, he was an idiosyncratic man with many singularities and paradoxes.

Last week, I arrived in England after a long, tiring trip during which I examined some Incan artefacts in Peru. The objects were chipped and full of fissures, yet they retained a beauty which only the relics of our ancestors have. One of them, a small statue shaped into the likeness of one larger ball and one smaller back connected by a bar, especially piqued my interest. Whilst most Incan bas-reliefs and artefacts I examined were simple and straightforward, I wondered at what meaning this one signified. The following day, I went downstairs for a cup of coffee and chanced upon Wilhelm sitting alone and looking thoughtful as usual. I made myself comfortable and told him of the old fragments of masonry that we recovered; when I mentioned the circular object, his excitement was palpable. He started making strange inquiries as to the length, breadth, and height of the bas-relief, as well as the stone it was carved from.

I answered his questions with puzzlement, for the usually tepid, taciturn man had become suddenly garrulous and engaging. When I told him that the artefacts were now restored in the Cornicancha Temple, he excused himself hastily and almost leapt out of the café in joy. I scratched my head in amusement and curiosity; what in hell had come over him? I even considered calling a psychiatrist but refrained from doing so and went to sleep with a heavy heart.

After a short, distorted sleep that night—an hour or two at the most—I heard the deafening blare of an ambulance, followed by a rush of footsteps. I unlocked my door and saw that Mr. Derby's door was open. Cameras flashes were emanating from his apartment. As I approached his doorway, I saw a scene which is now engraved into my memory: Wilhelm sprawled on the floor, white, with his mouth open in horror and spittle drooling down his stubble of a beard. The forensics found no certain cause of death, and the coroner expressed his disbelief. It was not a toxin, certainly, as his blood was analyzed thoroughly; neither was it strangulation, as no cord-like marks engraved his throat. He was buried discreetly, with no attendants except for me, as he apparently had no friends or relatives.

Now readers, keep an open mind for the following events. Though some might question the relation of Wilhelm Derby's death and the following events, believe me; all the loose ends shall be tied by the discovery which fate chose me to find. Three days after Wilhelm's burial, I received an international call from Professor Sebastian Rodriguez of Nazca University, who helped considerably in the process of scavenging the Inca artefacts. He spoke with the utmost urgency to break the news of the mysterious destruction of the whole set of relics. The artefacts, supposedly, were shattered into small, fragmented slivers of their once-whole ... "bodies"? and one was missing—I am sure you know which one. I was at a loss for words and ended the call by giving the poor professor my warmest condolences and the best of luck.

The following day, I started organizing Derby's papers, for, of course, I was the only person entitled to do so. As usual, everything was neat, yet I helped by putting the papers into files and categorizing them. When I opened the last cubbyhole in his office, I found the papers which flipped my world upside down. The title was made up of incoherent runes:

♋ ❖ꞵ♌⊠□↗ꞵ□● •♑↗◆ꞵ

Inside, the papers were full of these strange runes. Did my friend belong to a cult? I took the papers home, and, summoning the deciphering abilities which helped me defeat the Egyptian hieroglyphs, I studied the language. Eventually, I began to understand the rhythm and pattern, and step by step, I translated the symbols into words and placed them in a coherent order. If translated literally, the verb would be at the beginning, the subject in the middle, and the object last. The process took me days, even though there were only a couple of pages. Here is my final result. Take a deep breath, a very deep one, and learn the secrets which shall change the very foundation of our world:

A Xypholian Study

I: On the Behaviour of Humans

We, as beings of science, remain baffled by a creature that has long been studied. The creatures, which reside on a planet called Earth—the twenty-first planet with biological life on it—have proven to be a peculiarity in more than one aspect. We, as the inhabitants of Xypholia, abducted certain specimens from all over the planet for well-nigh five hundred years; and yet still to this day, we don't have any firm conclusions regarding them. The beings presented unprecedented behaviour and strange mutations. Hereby, I, the Anointed of Xypholia, write this report in the futile attempt to study their wild, savage minds with certain evidence. Patience and time were the *condiciones sine quibus non* with which I studied them, and, as a long-living race, we have plenty of the latter.

Humans, indeed, are strange beings. All of the specimens that we abducted, whether masculine or feminine, had one common point: high intelligence. However, their rituals and the methods of 'education' have an uncanny ability to suppress the intelligence levels considerably. Moreover, humans are social; an individual must live with others in order to preserve his sanity. Paradoxically, those beasts pleasure in killing their own kinsmen to a flabbergasting degree.

II: Past Interactions with Humans

In the blessed year of 12810 ♍, when the beings lived in small parts of the planet, the Xypholish landed on Earth and managed to interact awkwardly with the inhabitants of a scorching desert with only a river to quench their thirst: Ancient Egypt. They regarded us as immortal deities, and called the anointed of that time Ra. As a gift, we honoured their ignorant king, their pharaoh, by building a vast, pyramidal sarcophagus with the sun illuminating his grave on his day of birth. We discreetly abducted two adults and their offspring in order to study them, and left the planet. In the meantime, another fleet of our spaceships landed east of Egypt and helped another civilization, which called itself Babylon, into flourishing. Our kin also built a gift for them: the Hanging Gardens of Babylon. I have read the testimonies of the so-called men of science of their race and found them wondering as to the method of irrigation, which, in turn, made them think that the gardens were purely legendary. We used an element found in Nianogana called ninoxycryptsoporium—a colourless, odourless substance with hydrophobic qualities—which relieves the plants of any need for water, nutrients, or photons.

Then, after ten ♍, about a thousand years, our cartographer detected a civilization living on a remote island that showed signs of civility and evolution. We interacted with them and taught them snippets of our considerable knowledge. Needless to say, they flourished and prospered greatly and called themselves the people of Atlantis. After a passage of two ♍, when the city was at its height, we sensed the threat that its people presented to the other 'Earthmen', and thus destroyed them by unleashing a semi-gelatinous beast called Frothmella. The beast still resides in the formidable Bermuda Triangle, sucking every fool who comes near its home in the sea.

After the destruction of Atlantis, we left Earth for a very long period.

III: On the Key of the Vault and Its Loss
When the ♍ War with the Centurial race flared up, Emperor Xynderia XI built a huge vault in which he stored all the information that our race had accumulated since the Great Explosion, and sealed it using a key made from Potenta stone. Xynderia constructed the

vault, because he believed that our usually peaceful race would stand no chance against the blasphemous Centurions, so he wanted to protect our precious knowledge from them. Soon after his death, we won the fight, eradicating the Centurial race; yet we needed the stored information in order to manufacture spaceships, weapons, medicines, et cetera. The key was in Xypholia, yet the vault was made in Potenta, and so we dispatched a large Vortex911 shuttle with fifty elite guards on board to transport the key. During the travel, a small military Centurial spaceship attacked. The Centurians destroyed the Vortex911, and our ship fell, along with the fifty guards, to Earth.

It seems to me that we are bound to Earthmen more than by fate alone. Ever since that accursed loss, our race began to degenerate. The secrets of our architecture and masonry were forgotten, and our other colonies in space rebelled after we lost our method of manufacturing weapons. Once the rebellions began, the Xypholish started sending our anointed to Earth to find the key to the vault.

IV: On a True Rarity
I hid in a land called England. Today a truly rare man called Henderson informed me tepidly of the retrieval of Incan artefacts. I made the usual inquiries about the relics, and did not believe my fake ears when he gave me the blessed description of the key. In an hour, my friends from Xypholia will release me from this mortal body I am in, and an unpleasant surprise awaits Cornicancha Temple.

****

Facts Concerning the Late Malcolm Henderson and His Papers
I, the Chief Inspector of New Scotland Yard, testify that no trace of Malcolm Henderson remains. From his words, I deduced that he

perhaps committed suicide; yet, even after a thorough examination, we did not find his remains. In conclusion, he either killed himself by drowning in the Thames River by Imperial Warf, or perhaps he was kidnapped by robbers. Perhaps.

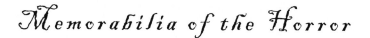

Memorabilia of the Horror

PART I:

The Horror in Keswick

CHAPTER 1

John's Journal
On the Arrival and
Other Things

How many tons of terror a peaceful country can hide, and what unfathomable secrets might lurk in its darkest places, only I truly know. It is true that I made my own mistakes; but a person cannot oppose what God has written for him.

A peaceful and placid country—that was the first thought my mind formed as Keswick slid into view. The houses were clustered randomly, and the peasants who worked in the outskirts of the village were uncivilized-looking. Most of them wore dungarees over a plain shirt. However, the green trees, plants, and pure lake en masse provided a very nice view.

I am sorry. I should have introduced myself more properly, as to not confuse my readers. I am John Montgomery, a boy of fourteen, with blond hair and blue eyes that speak of my pure Anglo-Saxon origins. My parents, baby sister, and I were travelling to Keswick, a small English hamlet. My father, a lawyer of some reputation, had a case there. He was obliged to ruffle through the papers of one

Helena Pierce, a rich woman who met an unexpected death. My mother and I were thankfully able to convince him of bringing us along with him.

The journey from our house in Cambridgeshire to Keswick took five full hours. We passed small forests and hiked our way over mountains great and small. Along the way, I spent much of my time reading a book titled *The Eye of the World*, by Robert Jordan; and from time to time, I was so overwhelmed by the scenery we were passing, I'd wedge my middle finger through the book and close it. The drive through the interwoven English highways was totally fascinating for someone who barely went outside.

When we entered the village, my father carefully drove through the narrow streets of the hamlet, stopping at a modern shop and entering it—'Cumbrian Cottages', it read. A stout woman shook hands with him and gave him a couple of keys. My father uttered a polite reply and exited the building.

The keys were for the villa we had booked previously. The villa was on the outskirts of the village. It was small and narrow, as English houses are doomed to be. Yet the house was furnished in a most modern fashion, and there were even some bookshelves with interesting titles on them.

The house was at the intersection of Church Street and St. Peter's Street. The first-floor corridor that went straight to a staircase. To the right of the corridor, there was a kitchen linked with a dining hall. The two rooms were quite big for a seemingly-small house. There were two bedrooms on the second storey, both furnished expensively and elegantly and with en suite bathrooms.

After unpacking our belongings, we went outside to break our fast. The village's main square, fortunately, was only a five-minute walk from our house. There we came upon a fish-and-chips restaurant, which we were very happy to find in a land of such isolation as Keswick. We ate in peace, with no one except us in the restaurant. My father tipped the youthful waiter, who, when asked about a good place to go to, replied, "Aye, sir, I do certainly know magnificent areas to visit. To start, there is the Grasmere Ferry Ride, where you'll ride a ferry across Grasmere Lake. There are five stops where you can disembark from the ferry, but you will have to wait for one whole hour until the next ferry comes to pick you up". A brooking look came over his face as he continued. "Sir, heed my words. Do not stray far; for here, in Lake District, there are secrets which man was never meant to know". With that, the young man went away.

With our bellies stuffed, our backs and thighs aching, we mutually agreed that the ferry ride should be delayed until tomorrow. We went home and spent the evening resting.

****

Interlude 1

[Taken from the Lake Gazette]
Common Abduction, or Something Deeper?
By Herb Simmons

Last night, a great commotion occurred in Keswick when a boy in his adolescence disappeared under ominous circumstances. Kaiser von Falkenberg, a teenager four years past his first decade vanished indeed in an obscure fashion. He was supposed to return from his grandparents' house—a-three-mile-walk from Keswick—at 8 p.m. His grandmother, an elegant woman in her seventies, stated that Kaiser obediently left her at eight exactly. When she dialled Mr. von Falkenberg an hour later, she was greatly alarmed by her son's anger over the adolescent's delay. The latter was the spark that ignited the current commotion.

Mr. Gladwell, chief inspector of the Lake District Police Department, expressed his disbelief at the boy's unpredicted disappearance. He stated that the police patrolled all the way from the teen's grandparents' farm to his parents' cottage without any sign of him. Later, police officers deployed dogs that made a remarkable discovery, finding a footprint in the malleable mud outside the grandparents' property. After a quick confirmation that the shoeprint did indeed belong to the boy, the police continued tracking the footprints. The prints became shallower and shallower as they entered Grasmere Forest. The ground there was hard and dry, as the densely packed trees of the forest protected the road's soil from being soaked with water. Thus, Kaiser's shoes did not make a deep enough imprint.

However, with the aid of dogs, the police were able to track the print deeper into the forest. A mile inside the pitch-black forest, the print disappeared completely. The relentless police dogs began turning in circles around the last visible footprint. No sign of the boy, either visible or invisible, remained.

"We *will* find him, no matter what", said Gladwell. "Even if the boy is in the nethermost depths of hell, we *will* find him".

CHAPTER 2

Mr. Montgomery's Memoirs
Century Manor

When the first rays of light pierced the black veil of night, the mobile phone resting beside me vibrated vigorously as it received a call. I stifled a yawn and mumbled angrily. For who, but a rude, uncaring person, would call at such an inappropriate hour? I grasped the phone between uncertain fingers and, with a short hesitation, answered the phone.

"Mr. Montgomery. Hello?"

The caller was my boss, Mr. Horton, the notoriously-merciless manager of the Horton Solicitors' Firm. Shaking the drowsiness from my throat, I managed to utter a proper reply. He told me that he was relying on me to finish the case with Miss Pierce today so that I would be able to attend a conference of considerable importance tomorrow morning. I was able to detect between the lines that a promotion was in order if I obediently fulfilled his orders.

Unfortunately, the Ms. Pierce's case needed days, if not a week, to finish. To start, I was obligated to find her will, her family tree (as to find the most rightful heir or heiress to her property), and any business-related papers. Add to that, I had to investigate fully her death, and to take her death certificate. I attempted to convince Mr. Horton with the latter arguments; yet, as he is my boss, he prevailed and ended the call by saying injudiciously, "Do not let me down, Harold". With that, the line went dead.

After going through my everyday morning chores, I went downstairs, where my son and wife were eating breakfast. I broke the bad news as sweetly as possible. They were outraged, so I said, "Fret not, Diana. John, stop whining. You know how important it is that I finish this case quickly. So here's the deal: you can go on the ferry ride, and I will go to Century Manor. I will probably stay there till evening. Then, I will scoop you up from wherever you are and return here, where we will rapidly pack our belongings and return home". They shared scowls between them as I ate an egg-and-cress sandwich and drank a lukewarm cup of tea.

After dispatching my family at the port of Keswick and giving them sufficient money for the ride, I drove quickly through the narrow, tortuous road that led up the mountain to Century Manor. I was not able to fully appreciate the beauty that surrounded me because of Mr. Horton's ill-omened call. My SUV hummed rhythmically as it sped across the slope.

I parked the car between shady groves and turned the engine off. The manor was a large, prestigious house built on the top of Mount Sheffield. Its back side hung precariously over a sheer, seven-hundred-metre-high precipice. It was painted a rich mahogany brown and had a solid Victorian design. My shoes scraped across the cobbled pathway as I walked over it.

I fished the manor key from my pocket and unlocked the large door that could allow entry for four men walking abreast. With a creak, the door swung open, revealing a spacious hall with a huge crystal chandelier. I closed the door behind me and locked it firmly. A dull thud rang as wood struck wood.

Dear reader, I shouldn't weigh your mind with useless details. So, moving on, I spent the first hour in Ms. Pierce's study, looking through her papers carefully. However, my thorough examination was met with disappointment, as no papers of relevant importance were there. I then left the room and consumed some of my preciously-dwindling time in finding her bedroom; for, in my opinion, if any will-related material was not found in a study, then a bedroom came in second place.

Like all of the rooms, Helena's bedroom was cavernous. It had a king-sized four-poster bed and many essential accessories. The walls were wallpapered with attractive, colourful hues. A crimson carpet dominated the floor, with a small chandelier in the ceiling. Truly, the room was immaculately designed. Adding to the former, the room had a view overlooking the precipice and what lay at the very bottom of the cliff. To begin, I searched her cabinet, yanking it open. Many dust-covered garments spilled onto the floor. I began folding and returning the clothes neatly when I noticed that one royal-blue skirt was a little stiffer than it should be. When I spread it, a cloth-bound book, coated in dust, fell to the ground. It was clearly a diary. I picked it up hesitantly, for it seemed wrong to read the private notes of a woman, even if she was long dead.

In the end, curiosity won over, and I opened the book. The first half of the year was filled with daily entries that were not of any significance to me, and so I skipped over them. After July, her notes were seldom and random. On the twenty-first of August, a week before the middle-aged woman's untimely death, there was a note that perked me up. I recovered the scrap of paper to my pocked. It read:

August the 21st,
  They came for me. Told me that I had to choose which way I want to seek: the path of the prey or the predator, the path of light or dark. They cut the electricity and all other means of communication. I am afraid ... O, God! Help me!

I was deeply interested. Had the woman been delirious or insane? Was she not fully *compos mentis*? What was this heretic piece of confusion? Who were *they*? I flipped the page. There were no entries on the twenty-second or twenty-third. On the twenty-fourth, she wrote an even more mysterious entry, which I also recovered, in order to put in Ms. Helena's case

24 August
  They have laid siege to my home. If not for my faithful bloodhounds, I would be rotting already. The moon is waning. Here I am huddling whilst the teratoid monstrosities are doing their forbidden rituals. What will they do to me? Why did I come here? Why?

The final entry was on the day of her death, the twenty-seventh of August:

27 August
  They are here, looking for me! My faithful dogs are ripped to shreds. There is no way of escape. May God curse this sheer drop which I once counted as a privilege. Hereby, I, Helena Pierce write my will:
  To the unfortunate solicitor who will be obliged to come here, may God protect you! My plea is of the greatest importance. Before those blasphemous deities engulf you, try to burn the house. I want no heir to meet my fate. Burn the house! Burn it. I hear their webbed footsteps on the stairs. Here they come.

CHAPTER 3

John's Journal
Just Like Chicken

After my father disposed of us at Grasmere Lake, my mother—who was pushing my infant sister's carriage—and I walked down the small port. We bought tickets for a ferry ride that started at half-past twelve. In the meantime, we fed the greedy ducks whatever leftover breadcrumbs we were able to find. The way in which the vividly-coloured creatures fought for a small crumb was indeed comical humour.

Beside us, a considerably-large crowd was waiting impatiently for the ferry to come over. Most of the people were elder men and women who had nothing to do in life except for sitting and waiting patiently. Retired people are indeed tactful; for as we approached the seats, the women parted in order to make a comfortable space for us. We sat shyly amongst them, and they started probing our history gently and with a hint of curiosity.

Finally, the ferry came to our rescue, and the thirty-or-so passengers disembarked from it. My mother held my baby sister whilst I folded the portable carriage. We went aboard the small yacht and made ourselves comfortable. After everyone was seated, a young woman in casual clothes explained the rules for the ride. Her manner was very cheerful as she told us that the ferry would stop at five mini docks. At each dock, the passengers were free to choose whether to disembark or stay on board. Again we heard that if we chose to get off, we would have to wait a full hour for the next ferry. My mother and I knew all of this, yet we listened patiently to her chatter. We planned to stop at dock C, the third dock, and continue from there walking—a thirty-two-kilometre walk—until we reached Keswick. It would be an arduous journey that, at least, would consume two hours and a half.

The engine roared to life. Water started frothing as the machete-like blades propelled the ferry onward. Soft, warm wind lashed at my skin, whilst tiny droplets of water splashed my face from time to time, refreshing both body and soul. Although the whirring of the engine was quite loud, the board did not move at the velocity one might expect. We passed trees of different hues and shapes, whilst we, as tourists, took photo after photo. After about five minutes or so, we reached dock A, where an elderly lot descended from the ferry.

Likewise, we lost about half a dozen passengers at miniport B. When we neared dock C, Mother and I started collecting our items and readying my sister's pram. Strangely, nobody except for us got ready to disembark at this dock. We climbed down from the ferry and started stretching our muscles, as we were about to venture on a trekking adventure in the wild countryside of Lake District.

The first stretches of land that we encountered were sparsely littered with trees and fern-like plants. Yet they offered a splendiferous complexion of nature at its wildest that overcame the crudity and simplicity of their components. The land before us was free of roads, so we were relieved of the presence of *die autos*. From time to time, we passed a farm, where a solitary farmer, or a couple by the most, worked silently.

We trudged silently. Paradoxically, time passed both quickly and sluggishly. For as my mother, sister, and I stopped before a natural feature that differentiated from the rest, time seemed to pass rapidly; yet when the recurring scenery ran unbroken around us, every step became an agony (exaggeratedly), as if our feet attempted to remind us that many more steps were coming.

It was after about twenty-seven kilometres of awed walking that a devilish idea popped into my mind. I believe that in every human being, there is a black spot of recklessness in his very core. If that spot of primeval instinct was not quenched and sated from time to time, it will suddenly explode when you need it the least (as is sometimes the case with me).

Thus, when noticing that my mother, who was ahead of me, paid me no heed, I retrieved my iPhone from my pocket, checked our location, and found out that after approximately a kilometre, we were going to reach a private farm on our left hand. The farm would cut the distance to Keswick short by a mile and a half. So, if I sneaked without my oblivious mother's knowledge, I could reach the town before her. I imagined myself leaning on a 'Welcome to Keswick' signpost whilst waiting for my mother.

When we approached the private property's gate, I checked that my mother was as absorbed as before with our surroundings, and with a barely-suppressed giggle, I pushed the rusty gate open. It creaked as the unlubricated hinges ground against each other. Closing the gate behind me, I looked over at what lay before me: a barn; a small house; and tall, gaping trees everywhere else. After a shaky, deep breath in a futile attempt to shake off my pusillanimity, I started walking vigilantly across the farm. Blackening clouds began obscuring the small glimpses of horizon visible between the sky-blotting trees as twilight descended.

The leaf-strewn path was intimidating because of the trees and the waning daylight. It gave everything a weird glow, which did not calm my ambivalent emotions. Then, about a hundred metres from the gates, I noticed a green and leafy oak tree which stood in contrast with the bald, naked trees everywhere else. Nearing upon it, I saw, to my surprise, a prophetic poem or whatever it is, carved upon its hardy trunk. If my memory betrays me not, the poem read thusly:

> *Eating a Soul renders Death sated,*
> *To delay the Line that was dated,*
> *The stronger the life, the stronger the Flame,*
> *Yet to endure the Stolen-from's blame,*
> *By the Light of life the eyes may get blinded,*
> *And the Almighty's wrath too, is rekindled*

I touched the carving with my forefinger. The callous bark was cool to touch, and drops of dew collected in it.

"Mesmerizing, isn't it?" a raspy voice asked from behind me. I looked quickly over my shoulder, where I saw an even more peculiar sight. Have you ever, avid reader, seen someone young with *old* eyes? I, myself, have always held to the belief that the only part of the human body that does not wither, even if its owner is in his or her seventies, is the eyes. They remain bright and shiny no matter how wizened you are.

However, there stood before me a woman in black, with stark-black hair. She looked quite young, an appearance betrayed by a hunch in her shoulders that only the elders have, and blue eyes that were *old*-looking. No attempt to describe her eyes would ever fully suffice in doing so. They had the glassiness of death. All in all, she looked in her late fifties.

She smiled pleasantly and presented herself as Mrs. Patricia Tanis. Instead of being conspicuous and outraged for my illegal presence, she invited me to her cottage in order to drink tea together. I rejected her invitation politely, and told her of my pressing needs. She remained intransigent, telling me that I had to come by and using her veil of widowhood as a talisman to persuade me. I took pity on the woman and accepted her invitation, remembering that my mother was still a couple of kilometres ahead of me.

I followed Mrs. Patricia to her cottage. She unlocked the door and led me to her sitting room, where she made me sit on a comfy yellow armchair. Her cottage was furnished plentifully and artistically. Her tastes were queer. Objects in varying shades of black dominated the house, as if she bought them to remind her of her widowhood. Moreover, the paintings on the walls depicted fights, and even one painting, by the grotesque artist Richard Upton Pickman, depicted a mysterious entity hunched over a man, eating him. I averted my eyes from the chilling view and looked at the coffee table in front of me, which held a platter of sandwiches.

She called her maid, one Isabella Sakharov, and ordered her with gentleness to make English tea for both of us. I was fidgety both with embarrassment and the desire to leave Mrs. Tanis away. She handed me one of the sandwiches, and said, "Eat it! I find eating a lovely chicken sandwich with lettuce very nourishing". I held the sandwich with uncertain fingers and gnawed like a rodent on its edges; I felt quite embarrassed by her hospitality. Then, seeing that I was making a fool of myself in front of her, I took a huge bite and savoured the taste.

How foolish I was! When the food settled deep in my stomach, an unprecedented dizziness crept over me. The world spiralled and collapsed before me, whilst the woman stared passively at me. I wanted to shout and shriek, yet my throat was constricted. Black spots danced before me, and I soon fell unconscious.

CHAPTER 4

Mr. Montgomery's Memoirs
Unwelcome Visitors
... Them or Us?

Strange it is how mortal men yearn for things out of reach, yet when it becomes available, they regret it. So was the case with me; for since Mr. Horton's ill-omened call, I have been doggedly looking for the will. Then, when I finally found it inside a finely-woven skirt of hers, with only one instruction: 'BURN the house! Burn it!' and nonsense about monsters and forbidden rituals from a diseased imagination, I almost lost consciousness.

I was obligated to tell Mr. Horton about my discovery, knowing the news would not put him in a serene mood. However, I left my mobile in my vehicle, so I thought to check if Ms. Helena's line was still working. I left the room and went to the main hall with the chandelier, which bathed the entire corridor in a soft light.

Dusk had long since fallen, and my hands stumbled when looking for the light switch. After a curse or two, I finally found it and switched it on. God knows that this simple movement, done by instinctual aversion to the dark, saved my life later on. I went down the stairs, where an old-fashioned telephone sat on a small brown table beside a window.

Picking it up, I dialled my boss's number. Fortunately, the telephone line was working. After a couple of rings, the other line came to life as Mr. Horton's usual reply came through the speaker. "Hello, Mr. Horton's Solicitors' Firm. May I help you?"

"Mr. Horton, it's Harold. I called to tell you I found Miss Helena's will. However—"

Suddenly, the lights from the chandelier died. The phone line went dead. The power must have been knocked out, I thought. I didn't know something paranormal was actually occurring. Just then, I saw the flicker of a dozen torches approaching the house outside, followed by obscure silhouettes of many figures.

Needless to say, the sight inspired a fear deep in me, and I sensed that whoever was hovering nearby the manor were no friends of mine. I placed the phone on the hook and tiptoed upstairs. From downstairs, the sudden sound of something bashing into the locked door rang through the house. I knew the manor quite well now, and soon realised that the only possible route out of this blasphemous house was Miss Pierce's bedroom window. My earlier search through the house revealed that the other windows were all barred with shutters as a safety measure. Miss Helena's vantage point over the cliff ensured her safety without the need to install bars in her bedroom.

I went to the deceased woman's room and took a closer look at the view overlooking the cliff. After a hasty yet careful inspection, I found that there were footholds I could use to get to the other side of the house.

Downstairs, I heard something being broken and then the muffled padding of feet on the carpeted hall. "Findst him!" a guttural voice said. "Let not that scoundrel escapest from thee!" I took a deep breath and lowered myself from Ms. Helena's windowsill. Her house's Victorian design helped me find footholds on the sedimentary stone with ease. Just when my head was barely hidden, I heard someone entering the woman's room. I silenced my breathing and clung desperately to the jutting stones. After a while, whoever—or whatever—was in the room left silently. I thanked God and resumed my descent.

After descending a couple of metres, I started edging to my right-hand side, never looking below me. There was a moment when I stumbled and thought myself a goner, but I was luckily able to catch the small ledge. If not for the light presented by the moon, I, Harold Montgomery, would have fallen certainly to my death. In the end, I was able to fully scale the wall and land on solid ground again.

My second step was to reach my SUV without alerting whatever strange beings were in the manor. I crouched and walked in haste. There was my car, parked in a shady place. I reached it and climbed inside, readying myself for the inevitable confrontation with those mysterious intruders; the sound generated by the vehicle's engine would surely alert them to my escape. I turned the key, and the engine came into life. I pressed the gas pedal, wove the car between the trees, and quickly flew down the road.

I glanced at the rear-view mirror one last time. There they were: figures with wide noses; flabby, pouty lips; large eyes that were entirely white; illuminated by the torches, which emphasized their bald heads.

CHAPTER 5

John's Journal
The Whetting of a Knife

I opened my eyes, disoriented and frightened. My mind was hazy, full of random, wild thoughts. Minute by minute, I regained coherence, and my vision became more vivid and defined. I remembered the poem, the woman, the sandwich. My limbs, which were first useless, became more obedient to my will.

I was in a bare room with one tiny barred window. The latter was the first coherent observation that my mind formed. Beside me was another boy who seemed to be my age. He was slumped against the wall with his head bowed. The boy had bright orange hair that only the Germans specialize in. I crawled over to the boy and shook him gently.

He woke up slowly. I asked him who he was and was greatly surprised when he identified himself as Kaiser von Falkenberg. I had read about the boy's disappearance. I pressured him with many questions regarding our whereabouts, yet he remained silent, no matter how much I urged him. When seeing that there was no hope in him, I retreated to a corner. The boy and I continued sitting in silence, punctuated by the occasional muttering from him. I was scared, and his muttering did not help calm my nerves.

About an hour after I realised that the so-called Patricia Tanis must have drugged, I heard the sound of a lock turning and swivelled to face the door. Two men entered the room. Both of them had white, filmy eyes and downturned lips; I called one One and the other Two. They walked arrogantly, their shoulders heaving up and down. I could hear the tinkle of metal in Two's pocket. Ignoring my presence completely, the two men went to Kaiser. He barely resisted them as they took hold of his shoulders and knees and hauled him away.

An unchivalrous idea popped into my mind. I stood up, faced Two, and lunged at him. He hadn't anticipated my feral attack, so I had enough time to tackle him. Then, with ease, he took hold of me and threw me with such force at the wall that it knocked the breath out of me. Silently, he left the room with his brother (or whoever One was) and poor Falkenberg.

After they locked the door, I unclenched my hand to reveal the object which caused my near-suicidal mission. It was a Swiss Army pocket knife, fully supplied with a corkscrew, a screwdriver, and (of course) a knife. Now reader, you might be wondering how in hell I was able to take hold of this knife. Suffice it is to say that when I jumped at Two, my sole purpose was to steal whatever metal was in the man's pocket, as I thought it might aid me in escaping from this house of horrors. Thus, during Two's disorientation, I was able to quickly pickpocket him.

With my heart thumping wildly, I walked toward the barred window. Judging from its width, I could squeeze through the window once the bars were destroyed. With renewed vigour, I started working on the six bolts which fastened the bars to the window, using the screwdriver. The bolts were rusty and corroded, and I had to put my arm in an awkward position in order to unscrew them. From a vent nearby, I heard sounds coming from the floor below me—something being whetted, sharpened, and shouts from the German boy. His cries reverberated through the house. I was awestruck as I fit the pieces of this mystery together, and a revelation dawned on me

The residents of this house were cannibals. They captured the stray and devoured them—God forbid that I should ever linger on what type of meat I ate—which indeed illuminated the mystery of the poem—if I were more careful!—and the abduction of the boy and me. Poor Kaiser. What were they doing to him downstairs?

Falkenberg's shouts were full of agony and fright whilst I sat working on the hinges of the bars. In a minute, I disposed of the first bolt and started working on the second. Downstairs, Kaiser's pleas of mercy became more subdued. The third bolt dropped with a rattling sound. No sound came from downstairs. The fourth bolt was unscrewed. A step upon the stairs—someone is coming for me! The fifth bolt I unhinged, and thus the bars, which relied on one hinge, collapsed.

Night embraced me as I jumped out of the window and into a small bush which softened my fall. My right knee was certainly bruised, yet I endured and ran as fast as my legs could take me. I looked over my shoulder, and I saw a scene which my unfortunate eyes will never forget: a misshapen lump with a butcher's cleaver sticking out of it.

From that moment, my journey with delirium began. Only small glimpses of that wild run remain in my memory. I remember shouting as loud as I could as I passed trees and shrubs. I remember passing a wooden hedge and the flashlights of a car blinding my eyesight. A familiar man pushed me into a car, wrapped a towel around my icy-cold body, and I surrendered to a sleep full of cleavers and terror.

When I awoke, I found myself in my father's dilapidated vehicle, with my mother beside him gently clutching my young sister. Light was starting to colour the sky with a bluish hue, and the accursed lake of Grasmere, which gave this district its name, was sparkling innocently. We were on a mountain pass which led out of the region. Just as the car turned, I gave one last look over my shoulder and saw Keswick: scenic, resplendent, and full of horrors. Asking my father about our destination, he replied, "Why, the Parliament House on Downing Street, and then home, of course".

****

Interlude 2
[Article from the *Guardian* Newspaper of London]

It is with hostility that the inhabitants of London and adjacent major cities regard the abductions currently under investigation by the Cabinet Minister with the collaboration of the MI7 and her Excellence the Queen in Lake District. Strangely, lawyers and human rights associations were hushed and silenced when they attempted to intervene. Only high-ranked officials of the government were involved in this highly-confidential operation.

Now for the reader in the dark, suffice it is to say (and these are the only details leaked) that the government assaulted the townsmen of Keswick in the dead of the night, kidnapping so many to the point of depopulating the hamlet almost completely. A humble guard of Downing Street came yesterday and testified that a ragged family stopped before the Parliamentary House and were greeted by the Prime Minister, William Saxton, himself.

The *Guardian* sent correspondents to Keswick, where we interviewed several persons, who all seemed relieved, by either saying, "Satan himself was taken", or by cursing and crying. We even dared break into a house, where we found congealed blood everywhere.

No matter what the government did, I believe that it is for the good of our country. And no matter what happened in Keswick, I will remain ever-loyal to my only solace and sanctuary.

PART II:

The Horror in Eynesbury

CHAPTER 6

Detective Noir's Notebook
A Recount of the Former

Ha ha! The insolence of fate! I, Private Investigator Noir of London, formerly of Paris, have been requited with the task of shedding some light on what has been termed to as the 'Keswick incident'! Why on Earth would I desert London, the mother of crime, and go to a small hamlet, you might ask. An explanation is in order.

The government has been very secretive and confidential in regard to the abduction in Keswick. Only the military's highest were involved. Even the constabulary is still left in the dark—and that caused the meeting with Norman Lansdale. Written below is my encounter with him yesterday.

I had been biting my fingers and tapping the desk impatiently, as if I instinctually knew the trepidation to come. A mug sat on the desk, black coffee residue staining its base. The air-conditioning unit was whirring restlessly, its rumble a sorrowful reminder of the luxuries I had been able to afford in the days of yore. The purple Victorian wallpaper was peeling in grisly patches, highlighting my current financial and economic standpoint.

I live in a claustrophobic two-storey house. The ground floor contains a corridor, which, if walking on a straight path, leads to a kitchen and its pantry. To the right is my office, which was originally a living room. I placed a black sofa outside my office's door in expectation of many clients to come. Opposite my office's door is a small bathroom. On the second floor is the cramped master bedroom plus a second bathroom.

Thus I was, tapping nervously, when the rusty bell rang. I lifted myself grudgingly, expecting the visitor to be the landowner or the electricity company. The boards creaked as I approached the door. And yet as I jerked it open, my expectations were disappointed. In front of me stood a man, well groomed and wearing a tight, formal tuxedo whilst carrying a brown leather briefcase. I smiled inwardly at the short stature of the man, and whilst shaking hands warmly told him to make himself comfortable.

I led the man to the office, and, taking his coat off, asked him if he would like a cup of coffee. He replied that he would indeed appreciate a cup. I left him in the office, and whilst making coffee contemplated how fortunate I was. The visitor seemed *rich*. And if he was neither the landlord nor the electricity company, then he surely was a client—a *rich* client.

Humming to myself contentedly, I entered the office and closed the door firmly behind me. The man looked up from his papers expectantly, and, scrutinizing everything around him minutely, introduced himself as Robert Nigg of the Human Rights Commission. With his nose raised high, he said, "Well, Mr. Noir, I rather find you the perfect person for this mission. With no offence, of course, I require someone lowly and discreet".

Then he briefed me with the mission. I looked at him in bewilderment as he told me what I was supposed to do. He told me that the HRC were not satisfied with the leaked information about the Keswick incident, and that my job was to go to Keswick as soon as possible to investigate the terrible secrets contained therein. When he finished his explanation, Mr. Nigg mentioned a six-figure number that was to be mine if the case was successfully completed.

With that, the man stood up and urged me with the utmost delicacy to keep the matter discussed confidential between the two of us. He excused himself.

Now, well, I am procrastinating.

CHAPTER 7

Detective Noir's Notebook
To Keswick ... and Beyond?

16 September, 11:45 a.m.

England is mostly composed of fertile green lands which are either domesticated, as in villages or cities, or left alone to grow wild and unscrupulous as doth a man's beard if he does not trim it. Upon nearing the north, the very nature of the terrain and the landscape changes utterly: trees grow up, and the churning gurgle of the fjords and streams become audible.

I became acutely aware of this fact as I sped through the interwoven, curved paths to my destination. 'Keswick in 5 miles', said the sign. I must admit, nocturnal driving does place a man on edge, with everything swathed in the veil of night. Brambles are visualized as lurking monsters, and fig trees, with their nude, thin bodies, create the image of stalkers. What a relief such a sign was! Five kilometres more and I would be snuggling softly in the bed of the inn I booked.

With a shaking hand, I turn on the radio. It coughed and sputtered static before focusing into slightly distorted voices. Strangely, the man on the radio was talking about the Keswick incident. I turned the volume up.

"The Prime Minister has called all news corporations to stop investigations in concern with the Keswick incident, says an insider source from the private meeting. Ha ha! What a cowardly movement, Mr. Minister! This is, ladies and gentlemen, what I term to as *euphemistic censorship*. We should give the government applause for performing their roles appropriately.

"Moreover, the Human Rights Commission withdrew from the mob of angry protestors yesterday. In his own words, Mr. Peter Smith of the HRA said, 'There is no evidence whatsoever of abductions occurring in Keswick, and as such, we shall not take any foolish measures chasing something intangible'. He refused to comment on the subject further. Indeed, I agree with him. No abductions occurred—just dozens of houses empty, a village depopulated, military barriers everywhere, and they say that—"

I turned off the radio. A maelstrom has been created by that incident. If my mind betrays me not, the whole crisis was sparked by a family that reported something to the ministry. If only I could find them.

After hours of driving past trees and shrubs, I suddenly found myself surrounded by a couple of small, neat houses, which were Keswick itself. I asked an old man walking his dog about the location of the local inn. He pointed toward a three-storey and saluted a goodbye. I drove over to the inn and parked. As I took my luggage from the trunk, a sense of foreboding enveloped me, only further accentuated by the foggy quality of the night.

My hands full, I kicked the door open. The reception was lit by a weak light bulb that gave the room an aberrantly reddish hue.

There were no sounds except for an electric fan whirring softly. I rang the bell on the desk. "Just a second, sir. Coming right now!" called a rather effeminate voice. A woman came down the stairs. She apologized for the inconvenience and bid me a good night's sleep as she handed me the keys. I thanked her and hastened up the narrow stairs.

Argh—I am drowsy! Not sure how I mustered the strength to stay awake this long, yet I figured that recording everything that happens in Keswick is of the greatest importance. Tomorrow is another day.

17 September, 09:15 am

Feeling refreshed and ready, I went downstairs early in the morning after fulfilling everyday hygienic rituals. For breakfast I had coffee and scrambled eggs. Everything went smoothly until a drunkard with sagging eyes barged in rudely and made a fuss. The woman from the night before kicked him out.

After eating, my main problem was the starting point for my investigation. *Where should I begin?*

I gazed at the innkeeper. She was cleaning the adjacent wooden table and humming. Stuffing a note in my pocket, I warily approached her. She looked up at me questioningly. "Yes sir?" she asked with a slight elevation in her eyebrows.

"Excuse me for asking, but do you happen to know about the abduction—no, I should rephrase it. What was the cause of the Keswick incident?" At the question, she glared at me and shrieked that if I were from the goddamned press, then she was going to throw me out of the building. Presenting my worthless business card to her, she sighed in relief, but nevertheless told me to shoo.

Handing her a few quid, the most efficient facilitator in the world, she changed her opinion mercurially. In a soft, ghostlike whisper, she told me that the whole issue was brought about by a family that had visited the village. "Next door is the office for Cumbrian Cottages, where the family supposedly rented a villa. Talk with the woman there". With that, she withdrew upstairs.

I exited the inn and inhaled a drought of cold, fresh air. The sun was ascending, with shadows shortening every second. My shoes made a muffled sound as I walked along the pathway. With a soft push, I entered the rental office. The building was floored with wooden planks and painted green on the walls. A stout woman in a skirt was rifling through portfolios. She glanced at me in disinterest and told that she could not lease me a cottage, as none were free.

Explaining my situation, I informed her that I just came to check her logbook, which she then reluctantly gave me. Opening her log, I looked at the first of September. Fortunately, there was only one entry: 'Montgomery, Harold; address: Cambridgeshire, Rosehip Road, 23'.

Interesting tidbit. However, Cambridge was about five hours away, so I thought I might as well investigate before leaving this place. Who knew what I was to find here?

After talking a stroll down Church Street, I found a fine-looking house with barriers preventing passage, reading, 'Military Intelligence—Do Not Interfere'. I looked around; no one was in the street. I jumped over the barrier and into the front yard. Weeds grew everywhere, their dank, soggy smell complemented by that of the aging manor.

Upon recollection of the horrors I found—which are still to follow—I find no answer to why I went to that house in particular. Keswick is not exactly a metropolis, but there are several houses throughout. Why didn't I go elsewhere?

Perhaps it was the physical shape of the house, or perhaps it was the aura of malice exuding from it, an aura that's darkness rippled in waves in gamma-like frequencies.

I approached the building carefully and ducked under the police tape hung across the doorway. The house's interior was drowning in dust. I found a small hall hung with eerie paintings. In one—which depicted a hunched humanoid eating a naked human corpse of a human—a poem had been written on bottom-left corner specifically, which I related, due to style and capitalizing, to before the Romanticism era of William Woodsworth. I took a photo of it as evidence. Here is the transcription:

> Eating a Soul renders Death sated,
>
> To delay the Line that was dated,
>
> The stronger the life, the stronger the Flame,
>
> Yet to endure the Stolen-from's blame,
>
> By the Light of life the eyes may get blinded,
>
> And the Almighty's wrath too, is rekindled

I studied the poem. What if the 'Line' was death? 'Eating a Soul [let us say, "the life of a fellow human", based on the painting] renders Death sated'. So, supposedly, eating a fellow human delays death, 'the Line that was dated'. Interesting …

The rest of the poem made no sense to me.

I tore my gaze from the painting and checked the kitchen—naught of interest. I then moved to the living room, which was rather lovely (though the aesthetic taste was old-fashioned). I went up the stairs to the second floor. It was composed of two bedrooms: one furnished overly (just as all English classic houses are), the other devoid of anything. It was as if the female owner, whose gender I guessed from the nature of the furnishings, compensated the emptiness of the second bedroom in the first bedroom.

The first bedroom was an ordinary one. However, upon entering the second bedroom, I found some bars upon the windows. They, except for one rusty nail, were unhinged. Was this room some sort of prison? Minute by minute, the reality of the house gripped me, and I realised the government's actions had been justifiable. A hideous picture was building in the back of my mind, yet my conscious section refused to accept it.

There was nothing more for me to do there, and so I left. Exiting the house, I glanced back. How illuminating that glance was! For though I am not the Creator, I can say for sure that, God willing, if I had not looked back, then I would not have participated in what has been termed the 'Eynesbury incident'.

I saw, beneath the stairs, a small door. Crouching, I entered it. It led to a basement. Sickly rays of sunlight filtered through very small horizontal windows. A cry escaped my throat. There sat a most commonplace table. However, there was … blood, deep, dark, pools of blood. I turned away and vomited. Not from the blood, not from the cleaver wedged deep into the light, absorbent wood—I vomited at the sight of a square chunk, a putrescent, decayed, fatty slab of meat.

To Cambridge! To Cambridge!

CHAPTER 8

Dr. Lamina's Epistles
Correspondence with
Dr. Hendricks

17 September

Dear William,

Hope that you are doing fine. I know that I haven't contacted you for a long time, but please forgive me. I have been very busy as of late. You might be wondering why I am sending you a letter in the twenty-first century.

The small sealed paper within contains tissue which I have collected from one of my subjects. No offence, but *why*, *how*, and *who* are none of your business unless the veil is lifted. I want you, William, to please analyze the skin and tell me if anything is wrong with it.

Warm regards,
Grace Lamina

18 September, 7:14 a.m.
Dear Grace,

Ha ha! Is this some sort of a trick? Did you take this sample from a mummy? The tissue you sent to me was about a century old. Not joking. The cells were dead. No cytoplasm. It must have dried up over time. The nucleus was so withered and wrinkled that further investigation was a prancing fantasy. I was thus required to dispense water droplets on the tissue so as to elongate it a little bit without causing a tear from within.

I am speechless. Who the hell are your 'patients'?

Répondez s'il vous plaît,
William Hendricks
P.S. Sending this email so as to reach you swiftly.

18 September, 8:03 a.m.
William,

Thank you for illuminating the truth. The sample which I sent you was actually taken from an *outwardly* youthful subject. That is all there is to know, as my lips, for the time being, are sealed. Please inquire no more.

For your best,
Grace

18 September, 8:15 a.m.
Ms. Lamina,

Excuse me. Today, I am going to finish some work-related material. Then, I am going to come straight away into Eynesbury to see what the [censored] is happening in there. Oh, yes, I am coming!

Concerned,
William

18 September, 8:18 a.m.

Sorry, William, but you won't be permitted to enter. I am terribly sorry if I awakened your curiosity.

Grace

Chapter 9

John Montgomery's Journal

18 September, 4:05 p.m.

Whenever in my deep heart the horror which we stumbled upon is about to be smothered by adolescent denial or imagination, some flashback breathes life into the horror. And with a loud howl in my inward ear, the truth comes out from the grave. My family is in a coma. My mother, the most fortunate of us all (apart from my little sister), resumed her normal life. My father, however, is totally different. To this day, I express gratitude to the Almighty that I am a teen; for as people develop, so do their intellect and reasoning. They formulate logical answers for everything and deny anything unknown, killing the flexible imagination. I, as a kid, still retain some imagination to the extent that I might be capable of believing in the paranormal, to devise some uncanny, mystic explanation, and to believe it.

My father, on the other hand, is a middle-aged man, as stripped from imagination (as all lawyers are, I believe) as a birch tree is unclothed during winter. He is traumatized to his very core. Yet I am sure that time and memory will trigger his rejection mechanism, and soon the horror in Keswick will be nothing more than a ghostly eidolon appearing only in eldritch dreams. Dreams, after all, are when the mind is unrefined and full of limitless imagination.

Going to and from school every day with heaps of homework helped to divert my attention from the past events. Thus I was, stooped over a mathematics notebook when the bell rang at around 4 p.m. My father was not in our house. If he was, then I suppose that he would have shooed the guest away politely.

I went downstairs and opened the door. A man with a curled French moustache looked at me. "Mr. Montgomery's son, I presume?" he said. I replied sarcastically that no, that I was his sister. He inquired if my father was home, and I found myself replying in the negative yet again. He asked if I could admit him, just to answer "a few questions of trivial importance". I told him to wait a moment, and fetched my mother. She welcomed the man, who apparently came from the government. He told my mother that he wanted to have a fast chat with me privately. She furrowed her eyebrows sceptically, but agreed, scuttling away to make some coffee.

I glanced at the man. He was sweating uneasily. He told me that his name was insignificant and outlandish anyway. He asked me, bluntly, about what happened in the town of Keswick. I looked at him as if he had slapped me in the face. I told him that many things happened to me, which I was not looking forward to narrating, and that if he was (as he claimed) from the government, then he would have been fully informed about everything which happened as of late. He coughed and said that our testimony was required again.

I wriggled uncomfortably and nodded sombrely. I told him everything, from the waiter's warning to the delirious journey to London. I even narrated my father's part, were he discovered that some Ms. Pierce was killed by the inhabitants of Keswick so as to hush her about their cannibalism.

Just as I uttered the word 'cannibals', the man nodded vigorously, as if consulting with himself. His hands trembled in excitement, as if saying "Oui, goddammit! I knew that something was devious!" I finally concluded by saying that the townspeople were divided—in consultation with Mr. Pierce's diary—into predator and prey. The predators fed upon the oblivious prey.

The man—whoever he was—stood up and thanked me. He told me if I knew where the mad cannibals had been consigned to. Forthrightly, I told him that, based on the Prime Minister's assurances, they were entrusted to an asylum nearby Keswick. He kissed my cheek in French fashion and told me with a wink that the greatest mystery of all was yet to be solved—the mystery of mysteries. The battle between predator and prey was imminent. He told me that as long as the poem was unresolved, there are still horrors to come. "The devilishness of the Keswickians was miscalculated. I must take action quickly".

The man excused himself and hurried out of the house. My mom came with the coffee. I, taking a cup from her, notified her of my deed. "You did what?!" She looked at me, horror-struck. Oops! I forgot that I was not supposed to speak about Keswick.

PART III:

The Drawing of the Three

CHAPTER 10

Trials and Tribulations

11:02 p.m., Dr. Lamina

I was sitting contentedly on my chair, rifling through the reports when I heard the *click*, followed by the reverberations of metal grating being pushed. *Silence ... tick tock ...* then *BOOM!*

They are pounding at my door!

Without my habit of locking my office when working in the hours of darkness, I would have been killed or devoured by now, had fate chosen to take a detour from the thoroughfare of events that occurred.

My speculation of the noises heard before was that, somehow, the monsters were able to unbolt the locks on their doors—*click*. The grinding of metal was caused by the bars sliding off—*sleeeet*. They must have crept mutely so as to ambush me whilst I was still unawares—and then *BOOM!*

What am I supposed to do? O God, sooner or later the door is going to collapse.

18 September, 10:21 p.m., Dr. Hendricks

I drew near the gates of Eynesbury's Asylum. From time to time I was obliged to spew some water on the windshield and swipe it with a cloth. It was very cold outside. The weather was temperamental as of late, always changing, to no one's benefit. The gates were open—well, not open, but unlocked anyway. I pushed the gates open and returned to my vehicle. Strange that no one was keeping watch. The government has been lethargic and sloppy lately. I drove into the gates.

Skidding across the tarmac, I parked the car directly in front of the main headquarters of the asylum. The institution was a sprawling compound of many buildings, comprised of employee residences, offices, and cells where patients of varying mental deterioration were kept. If I had not visited the place before, I would surely have been overwhelmed—and, to a certain degree, frightened. The lights were off—most peculiar. For God's sake, it was only 10 p.m.

I advanced upon the building. The revolving door was not working. I looked at my reflection in the glass and saw something behind me. Too late.

18 September, 10:23 p.m., Detective Noir

The time has come. I, whilst navigating the dark highway to Eynesbury, opened the glove compartment. There was a black box with the letters 'S&W' on it. I laughed nervously. Opening it, my hand grasped a lovely Smith & Wesson revolver. I placed the pistol in my pocket and grabbed a handful of bullets. The metal was as cold as death.

Finding Eynesbury was not a difficult task. It was the only sanatorium in the vicinity. I stopped in front of the gates and killed the engine there. Getting out of my car, I grabbed a torch, just in case.

Why all of these precautions? I discovered that the man-eaters were planning to pull a stunt like this, by means I will keep to myself only. Suffice it to say that the square of meat in the room under the stairs hinted so to me.

My breath misted as I exhaled. Pooh! My feet scraped along the asphalt with muffled sound. The gates were wide open. The gargoyles perched on either side looked like sentries. The asylum was quiet … too quiet to be natural. A car was parked right in front of the asylum's main office. I walked briskly, the September wind lashing my face.

A terrified scream echoed out, and I saw the silhouette of a humanoid figure leaping upon something. What, I could not see, as my view was blocked by the parked car. I maneuvered around to see a rabid person jumping at a neat, tall figure. The figure, which was actually a man in formal clothes, screamed and tried in vain to push the humanoid figure out of the way, but to no avail.

I pulled the revolver out of my pockets and aimed the muzzle at the monster. I closed one eye in concentration and pulled the trigger. *BANG! BANG!* The shots rang out through the silent hospital.

18 September, 10:27 p.m., Dr. Hendricks
BANG! I felt the creature upon my shoulder collapse. I threw it off my body and grimaced, feeling sick. There was a man standing in front of me with a peculiar-looking peculiar moustache. Smoke billowed from the muzzle of his gun. I smiled. "Thank you. That was most timely".

The man shrugged, shook hands with me, and introduced himself as Noir. Strange it is how men sometimes, even in the direst of circumstances, will still uphold tradition and courteous customs. I introduced myself quickly. Noir went to the fallen body and kicked it. "So this is what those unorthodox monsters look like", he muttered.

I asked him for clarification. He shook his head and told me that we should seal the asylum and leave as quickly as possible. "And as for those people who run the asylum", he added, "may they rest in peace". I pleaded with him to investigate into someone I cared for, Dr. Lamina. He shook his head and said, "Those beings"—he pointed at the beast—"have overrun the place. They, my friend, are the kidnapped subjects of Keswick, who the whole world thought were poor citizens and sought to defend them".

I was awestruck. Everything made sense now. So this is where the Keswickians had been hidden, away from the eyes of the world. However, I was still unmoved. "Please", I said, "just give me the gun, and I will go into the building myself". He smirked at me and said that the gun was not registered, that is, illegal. I gulped. When I informed him that the person I was looking for was, in truth, the supervisor of the rehabilitation of those beasts, his demeanour changed.

He nodded, and so I led the way into the dark abyss of the asylum.

CHAPTER 11

The Web Draws Tighter

18 September, 10:47 p.m., Dr. Lamina

There are about three beings pounding at my door. The others who crowded around the door disappeared, each with his or her—sorry—each with *its* own blacklist of people to kill. Those three were unrelenting. They've been hammering at the sturdy door all this time. I peered below the door and met two shining black dots. The lunatic looked at me through the keyhole. He—it growled and fetched a metallic chair—one of the many scattered around the asylum—and started ramming with unending vigour.

BOOM! BOOM! Screeeetch! The bolt is bending! God! What can I do? The knife, the surgical knife—where is it?

18 September, 10:50 p.m., Detective Noir

The hall was quite messy. I have expurgated the gruesome details so as to provide a more readable testimony. Saying that we passed several human corpses will suffice, people with whom my poor comrade Hendricks seemed to be acquainted; for several times he stopped near a body and uttered the person's name in a soft, stricken voice. A couple of bodies were missing chunks of flesh on their faces; others' ribs were poking out like raw rib-eyes.

Hendricks' eyes shone strangely as he led me from one corridor to another. Just when we reached the fire exit stairs (for the elevator was not working—no electricity), I heard the indecipherable growls of one of those insane cannibals. I stole a glance at it. The beast was, in fact, of average human size, but they had a noticeable hunch in their shoulders and a bending in their knees that made them look like apes—that is, unless you saw their demoniac faces.

I pulled my gun and removed the safety. Hendricks lowered my hands with a look that said to leave that being alone, for fear of alerting the others to our presence. I watched with disgust as the being crawled away into another room. We then tiptoed up the stairs carefully and soon heard the sounds of bashing nearby. Some of the beasts were trying to break into a locked room. Hendricks looked alerted and sprinted as quietly as he could manage. So I did as well, running in unison with him.

18 September, 10:56 p.m., Dr. Lamina
CRASH! The door fell like a wounded bear. I was standing behind a filing cabinet, of sight. The three figures entered slowly, taking their time. After the dust settled, they searched for me through the debris suffocating the room. I held my breath and clutched the knife tightly in my numb hands. A moment later, one of the beasts flipped over the filing cabinet. He—it looked at me maliciously, and lunged!

I, in a frenzied mania, drove the knife with such adrenaline that the blade sliced through the beast's trachea like cheese. The creature fell with blood gushing out of its neck like a fountain. I huddled and screamed and screamed and screamed.

11:00 p.m., Detective Noir

The screams of a lady echoed through the building. Hendricks shouted, "Lamina!" and started running as if the devil was following him. Across the corridor, we saw a door-less room from which hellish sounds were emanating. I pulled out my firearm and grasped it forcefully.

Bursting into the room, I found two beasts pushing and pulling barbarously at a poor woman. I pulled the gun and shot one right in its blighted head. The other beast retreated frightfully; and I, with a grimace, shot it mercilessly. It fell, black blood oozing from its head. The damsel in distress kept screaming, but Hendricks managed to calm her. He brought her to her feet and then said to me, "Let's run—quickly!"

The beasts had congregating in private business in a corridor. Each was minding his own victim when a deafening *BANG* rang out. They looked at each other in perplexity. *There is prey there*, they said. *Let's kill them. Letsus killst them. Run, lest thine prey escapest!*

CHAPTER 12

Valiant Acts

11:08 p.m., Detective Noir

I took off running as fast as I could. Hendricks and the doctor followed me step-by-step, and by that I mean sprint-by-sprint. Beastly sounds called from outside the asylum through the windows. They were coming. I descended the stairs in haste, my heart pumping like a maniac. "Not from here! They are coming from this way!" the doctor said, pointing at the corridor I was planning to venture through. She gestured at the other way. We took off in the other direction.

Emerging from the fire exit, I found myself on the grounds behind the asylum. It was empty outside. Panting and gasping for breath, I told my two companions that my vehicle was just outside the gates; we could make it out with our lives. The doctor intervened, telling me that we had to lock the asylum, thus securing the beasts from escaping. I told her that securing our lives was much more important. Hendricks took a neutral stance.

11:14 p.m., Dr. Lamina

Pointing to the small technical box in the backyard, I strode determinedly and ushered the two men in. Electric buttons filled the metal box, but I was well versed in the asylum's protocol and could easily recognize them. I looked at the two men and told them that, once I flipped the switch, we would have about thirty seconds before the main gate closed and the whole fence became electrified.

I gulped nervously and pulled the switch. "Run!"

11:14 p.m., Dr. Hendricks

I ran and ran and ran. Sweat poured from my skin as richly as a river. My heart burned with pain. Adrenaline flared, washing over my senses. How I would have appreciated a cup of water then. Ah, how strange humans are! That of which we are abundant we depreciate, and lust with fervour after that which we seek! And no more than a couple of usages, and we are depreciative again.

The gate was nearer with every step we undertook. Soon it began closing shut. Noir and Lamina passed through the gate first, and I, as always, took the rear. We hastened to the vehicle. Noir awakened the engine, reversed the car, and drove as if the devil was on him. I looked back at the asylum. The metal fence was buzzing. The gates had closed, and the electricity was running through the whole of it. I closed my eyes and took a shuddering breath.

****

Interlude

[Top Secret Document] Note to Prime Minister

Court officials announced today that the lives of the Keswickians are to be mercifully ended by the headsman after the astronomical costs of their devilry for the benevolent British government. Dr. Lamina, the doctor responsible for the cannibal psychopaths, declared after rounding up the psychos that, of three scores, only one lunatic is missing. To that, we must admit that it is miraculous that only one escaped—no doubt due to the valiant acts of Mr. Noir, Hendricks, and Lamina whom you met today. Her Majesty insists that the trio is to be crowned with honorary titles, without the knowledge of the public, for aiding in social security. The same goes for the former Montgomery family who exposed the cannibalistic disease from the beginning.

The precaution which her Majesty's office wishes to convey is the treatment of the victims of the Eynesbury incident. Their silence must be bought under any conditions or circumstances, for most of them entrusted their loved ones under our governance. The deaths exceeded a hundred by a few.

Hopefully the maniac who escaped has drowned in one of the bogs scattered around Eynesbury. Hopefully.

EPILOGUE

John Montgomery's Journal

I am sleepless. Insomnia tickles my senses, although the general exhaustion of today has rendered my muscles sleepy. It is silent outside—well beyond midnight, that is. I closed my eyes again, attempting to force myself into sleep, yet to no avail; for sleep, and what lies beyond it, is outside the reach and understanding of humans. My throat is parched.

Grunting to myself in irritation, I slithered out of the bed and flexed my muscles. Trudging down the stairs, I noticed a strange atmosphere in the house, menacing and evil, no doubt influenced considerably by that godforsaken trip to Keswick. My bare feet scraped against our carpeted floor. I entered the kitchen and filled a cup with water.

Back upstairs, I turned on the computer. My father's email account was open. A message with the subject "XXX" flashed onto the screen. I clicked on it and read its contents. It was sent by one Noir, and in it was written a well-known poem.

Eating a Soul renders Death sated,
To delay the Line that was dated,
The stronger the life, the stronger the Flame,
Yet to endure the Stolen-from's blame,
By the Light of life the eyes may get blinded,
And the Almighty's wrath too, is rekindled

Dear Mr. Montgomery,

Knowing that nothing induces fear more than ignorance, and keeping in mind that the brain is in turmoil as long as there is unresolved conflict, I am sending this message to tell you about the meaning of the poem. Had we all been in a more vacant state of mind, it would have been easy to derive that by rituals unknown those cannibals devour their fellow humans in order to sustain their life force and delay death. Such information is to be kept away from the world, for if people knew that cannibalism impedes death, we would face unimaginable consequences, the nature of which causes me to be sick.

Continuing on, the more youthful the cannibals' prey, the more life the cannibals gain. However, such a gift is not without a price, for the cannibals are deprived from humanity, existing in a state of total mental and physical deterioration.

Their so-called madness, which assaulted them *just*—yes, with emphasis on the word *just*—as the police imprisoned them was certainly a ruse to trick the innocent hearts of the jury and the judge, thus condemning them to an asylum instead of the guillotine. However, they surely were mad to some extent before.

Yours faithfully,
Noir

I grasped my head in amazement. So this was the meaning of the poem I read on that fateful day. If only I had known!

My head rocked back in surprise as a dull *thud* broke the silence of the night. Someone was knocking on the door outside. It was a strange sound—a muffled, monotonous scraping on the door, more animal-like than human.

I ignored it at first, but it is insistent. I think I am going to go open the door now. I wonder who it could be.

Beyond the Spectacles

How can black be white and white be black! Ladies and gentlemen, we are on the brink of our fragile existence, and not indeed on any grounds of scientific calculation whatsoever. These papers in your hands will be considered satirical and ridiculous by the majority of readers, no doubt due to the unique—and, to a certain degree, unbelievable—material contained within. Any scientific details of Heisenberg-level difficulty has been expurgated from these papers for two reasons: the first being that my aim is to appeal to a greater audience, for the intellectually-driven are narrow-minded, unable to grasp that which is out of proportion. The second reason is that the demographic profile to which I have dedicated these papers to is amateurish men of science who seek to follow my steps, lest they lose their sanity.

Do we not in our eldritch dreams envision traversing the abyss? Do we not dream of defying the laws governing us and roaming the universe? Have we not, whenever in a vacant mood, sought excitement in imagining the existence of other races similar to Homo sapiens? The irony, as I perceive it, is that we jump to speculations galaxies away, ignoring the wonders presented by our own world. The latter theoretical argument has been produced with the benefit of hindsight, that hindsight which caused the death of my colleague,

George Gordon, and the portentous inferno which engulfed Gonville and Cause College of the University of Cambridge.

I was adopted in my eleventh year since birth by one affluent Allen Dumas. Before that I had been the subject of fostering, and it is of note to say that during my foster travels, I met most unsavoury folks who infected me with their bad habits. I began smoking by age 12, and soon afterward I deteriorated to drinking beer from my adopted father's small refrigerator in small quantities.

And yet the craving could not be fulfilled! My father—who was sterile—was as oblivious as ever, believing his only son to be angelic. How I laughed with my friends! It all started with a bad mood and a smoky puff, upon the urging of a godforsaken friend (though I feel compelled to write 'fiend'). I kept going down the stairs of degeneration, believing myself foolishly as the 'coolest' man in the world. How ignorant was I!

After high school, where I performed fairly, my father told me that he expected me to be admitted into Cambridge. I looked into his face and laughed. Cambridge—who could enter Cambridge? I am sure that money exchanged hands somewhere, for I was extremely gobsmacked when they made me an unconditional offer. That was my turning point. University life changed me completely – the earnest faces, the audible 'please' and 'thank-you' manners affected me deeply. I started chasing after scholarly pursuits earnestly. Soon enough I met one of the most interesting people in my life, George Gordon.

George Gordon used to propose his wild assumptions in the Hall of Residence to fellow colleagues, usually in concern with the intangible line separating psychology from physiology, the *Beziehung* between being and the five physiological senses. He suggested that our reality is assumed by perception and touch only—taste, audibility, and scent being complementary to the latter. In explanation, Gordon said that the sightless form speculations based on touch; and if they were further deprived from touch, their existence would be well-nigh amoebic. If we were to breach either the wall of perception or contact, we would be able to engage with the Infraworld. Changing what we touch would require delving into the composition of our very sensory cells. However, changing what we perceive is much, much easier. In his later speeches, he theorized the existence of the Unnameables: invisible entities we can neither perceive nor touch, but can hear and smell in places of death and decay. He finally proposed the construction of goggles which could enable us literally to see different radiations within the electromagnetic spectrum. For example—and I must highlight that this is only an example far-fetched from *our* terrible reality—our eyes can only see light. We can see neither infrared waves nor ultraviolet radiation. His 'goggles' were supposed to enable us to do so.

Gordon's theories were largely considered insane. One day, after a particularly weird 'sermon', I went up to him and expressed my interest in being of assistance to him. We began working together on the spot, and soon occupied the physics laboratory. The university supplied us with all the resources we might need, from lenses to piezoelectric contraptions. We worked earnestly and into oblivion. We worked for months, telling no one except the higher administration of our progress. By this I hint to readers that hard work is always required to reap juicy fruits, for nothing just awaits harvest day without being sown in the first place.

The day before yesterday was *the* day. Adjusting the goggles to enable perception of waves, Gordon and I, using trial-and-error, finally settled on the frequency we believed to be scientifically accurate (which I will not write here for fear of being imitated by foolish people). As Gordon was the one who worked the most, I gave him the honour of trying the spectacles first. He grinned wickedly, and, punching me in the shoulder, placed them over his eyes.

Ladies and gentlemen, mark my following words carefully, for through their dazzling brilliance the mystery of the rumours of the late Gordon would appear to be solved. He placed the spectacles on his eyes and gasped audibly. "Oh, if only you can see, Dumas! Such ... ugh ... such splendour!" Gordon looked at his hands and flexed them. He was literally jumping up and down literally—that is, until he went to the window.

To this day, I do not know what Gordon *saw* exactly out the window. In the beginning, he was still as gay with excitement as before, jumping everywhere. Then his jaw dropped open, his skin paled as he uttered a scream, and his body became rigid with fright. With a cry, he tore off the goggles and threw them aside, storming out of the lab.

All of the aforementioned, ladies and gentlemen, happened before my very eyes. I stood confused for several moments after he left the room. Soon I forgot about the experiment and the goggles; all of my focus was on Gordon. I searched for him the whole day and night earnestly, going around the campus and asking my colleagues for any sign of him, with no luck.

I never expected what was to come. I never expected him to hang himself—as the discoverer of the corpse, a janitor, said after finding him the next morning—in a storage room. Gordon tied a rope around his neck, seemingly, and kicked the chair out from under his legs.

His funeral was yesterday. Nobody came, save for some far-away relatives of his; this was, no doubt, due to the considerable detestation he drew from people. The reverend spewed much religious nonsense. These folks are only efficient for leading the crusades; otherwise they are profoundly spurious. I once heard one of them, whilst over the grave of a criminal, say, "We are born in sin. We die in sin. Perhaps our fellow has done nothing, for we misjudge". It also happens that the 'fellow' has died from gunshots to the neck after committing armed robbery. I barely suppressed my clenched fists until the end of the sermon.

Today, when reason returned to my mind, I speculated on the cause for all of this lunacy. I was determined to clean out the items Gordon and I had left in the lab. Entering into the laboratory, I started ruffling through the papers scattered around the desk. Ducking under the table, I saw them—the damned spectacles. They were on, the machinery within humming quietly. I had forgotten them almost completely! What a moron was I!

The thing which subjugated Gordon to his demise was in my grasp. The concatenation was more than obvious: whatever Gordon saw, it was the key to solving the mystery. Ladies and gentlemen, I am procrastinating, lengthening my words histrionically, all in the attempt to prolong the time before I jump out of the window into the sequestered street below. I have suffered since that day from pains, just like the torturous borborygmus of the dyspeptic, and you shall now why.

I placed the goggles on the bridge of my nose, and blinked several times—total blackness. Were the spectacles not working? Could he have committed suicide just because the spectacles did not work? Impossible. He saw something for sure, otherwise he would not have been prancing the lab in excitement. I brought my hand in front of my face and uttered a scream. Great God! My hands—the skin, that is—were black, but the outlines of my hands were white. Everything in the room looked similar: the desk, the table, even my fingernails—all were mercilessly black with white edges.

There was an eerie sort of beauty in everything, a phantasmagoria of blacks and whites. *Wow!* I told myself. *Is this how things look if perception is altered from one sort of radiation to another? Such dazzling beauty!* Never did I realise that, with each step, I was taking myself toward the window, toward my oblivion. When I advanced upon the window, I saw a strange image which I describe below.

The view was blocked by many disproportionate cylinders, each about six metres in length, and with a diameter of about two metres and a half. Each cylinder had five protrusions in the likenesses of heads. In some cases, the heads—or whatever they were—increased in size and length from left to right; in other cases from right to left. All of this I took in with utter bewilderment. What were these cylinders?

Then I gazed up high into the heavens. As the true nature of the cylinders revealed itself, I shrieked in fits of hysteria and felt my throat constrict in fear. I wrenched the goggles from my eyes, and unlike Gordon, I broke them with a single stroke of adrenal rush. I gathered my things and, taking the Bunsen burner, ignited the laboratory and fled.

Ladies and gentlemen, you must be wondering about the stupendous nature of the cylinders with their five protrusions. How true were Gordon's ravings! Well, those cylinders *were just the merest paw.* The window! The window!

Ravings

What devilish, demoniac rituals our ancestors engaged in I dare not articulate; yet I saw a glimpse on the fifteenth of December which fully quenched my thirst for any such relevant knowledge. There is peace of mind in ignorance, in the unawareness of the horrors perpetuated through history. I, however, have been enlightened as to a horrible truth whose nature awakens nightmares whenever the moon, fully round, shines. I may have preserved some peace of mind through the flickering hope that the occurrence on the fifteenth had been nothing but the ravings of a drunkard. It is of note, however, to say that on that particular day I was as sober as a judge.

The reader must surely have heard of, or even seen, the standing stones of Stonehenge. They stand in the southwest of England, sprawled in an area called Amesbury. I will spare you a lecture on the erection of the stones in the Neolithic Ages by the mysterious peoples of that time. There is an infamous, lesser-known monolith known as Woodhenge by the woods of Amesbury, only a couple of miles from Stonehenge. This sacrificial henge was discovered in 1925 by one Alexander Keiller, and since then has been the subject of numerous studies and excavations. I have been involved with the latter, and this is where the connection betwixt the two comes into place.

Pardon the unseemly preamble. An introduction is in order. I am Doctor Neville Hastings of the Royal Archaeological Society.

In my childhood years, I lived in the countryside of Amesbury, in a small, homely cottage just around the corner from Woodhenge, separated only by a Catholic chapel and a stale meadow. Whenever I was in a vacant mood, I would abandon whatever inane occupation I had my hands in and swing by Woodhenge. There I would sit for what felt like eternity, mesmerized by the ancient relics whose purposes were, and are to this day, unknown.

From time to time, traffic from other Woodhenge visitors would block the single-way lane up the road. On these occasions, I would be nosier than usual, barging into their groups. Depending on the amicability of the visitors, I would then either be gently rebuffed or given a simplistic explanation of what they were doing there, which, to be frank, I understood nothing of.

Time has since passed, but there is no need to delve further into trivial details, as I find myself straying away from my purpose. A couple of months ago, spurred on by memories of childhood, I proposed to my colleagues at the Royal Archaeological Society a deeper, more extensive study into Woodhenge; for I believed that the wooden pillars could not have been created purposelessly. My proposal was approved, and I started working on the spot. And the date that I chose? Yes, the fifteenth of December.

****

It was windy. The ground was covered in a white blanket of snow, and the sun was locked in the middle of the sky, its fires giving off a reddish, subdued light like dying embers. It made quite the melancholy scene. Coughing audibly, I parked the car in front of the gate to Woodhenge. I then retrieved my equipment, consisting mainly of a photovoltaic lamp (which charges its battery by capturing sunlight during day), food, and a shovel (for exploring purposes). The wind was roaring, and brittle flakes of ice were swirling everywhere, blurring my vision. I attempted to warm my hands by rubbing them vigorously, to no avail. I even considered turning back home, yet I had business to do.

The snow crunched beneath my feet as I trod over it, its sound like the peal of crushed bones. Unlatching the lock, I opened the gate and walked into the henge. Taking in the beauty of my surroundings, my eyes lingered over the symmetrical wooden pillars, the tall grass, the trees, and the huge circle the wooden pillars made in the centre of the henge. I fished my notepad from my bag and started taking notes.

That's when I saw it, a mound that was noticeably higher than any surrounding terrain. It was in the very centre of the henge. Looking around me, I brought forth my shovel, approached the mound, and dug in. Bringing up dirt and throwing it aside, I kept shovelling until I confirmed my suspicions. There in the ground lay a sepulchre. Removing the lid, I found a skull, grinning at me toothlessly. Its hair still stuck in grizzled patches to its temple, but it was in such a state of decay that I averted my eyes in disgust. This special placement of the corpse meant only one thing: it was part of a ritual, a disgusting, abomination of a ritual.

Placing my notebook beside me, I crouched and squinted at the skull. The sun was dying behind the hills, giving off a weak, useless radiance. The cranium, which I handled with great care, was diminutive, as if belonging to a child. It was intact—that is, except for the edges worn by time. The parietal and suture regions of the skull were shorter than normal, giving the facial features an apish, bestial quality. This confirmed the theories that our ancestors had smaller brains with comparably limited capacities.

There in the naked wilderness, with the freezing wind lashing at my face, a sense of stuporous drowsiness washed over my senses.

It was as though the frozen mist in the air were dampening my senses and distorting reality. I buried the skull in its sepulchre, and standing up, went over to a naked fir tree and rested my head against the cold bark. *Only a moment*, I thought. *Just to rest.* The sun well-nigh vanished, and the land, once patched with silhouettes, became one seamless shadow. I fumbled in the darkness for the lamp and turned it on. The light was feeble, yet capable enough of throwing shadows everywhere. I hugged the lamp for warmth, and slept.

Whether that sleep was induced by the physical exertion of digging or the numbing coldness I do not know, yet I have theorised far more terrible explanations whose incomprehensible nature forbids me to tell. Nevertheless, be it sleep or incantation, I am ashamed of my siesta.

I woke to the sound of blasphemous chants and the wind echoing in the henge. Still bleary from my nap, I beheld a landscape swathed in mist. The lamp was long since dead. I attempted to stand; but just as my feet were about to take my weight, some force crippled me, and I fell on the ground again. My hands I no longer felt, and I am sure that, had light been there, they would have looked blue and lifeless. Terror seized me in its merciless grasp, rendering me handicapped in both body and mind.

The tempo of the chants increased, and with it, so did the wind's ferocity. Then out of the entombed earth they came—ghostly apparitions, resembling humanoid figures clad in furs and padded leather. They shone in their own iridescence, yet that radiance did not extend to the surrounding objects beside them, maintaining the clutch of the mist on the land. The phantasms floated into the air and commenced dancing in a weird manner. All the whilst they flavoured their dance with words from another tongue. It bore a great resemblance to English, but was more inclined toward a German barbarity of pronunciation.

All of this I watched with great perplexity and disbelief. Had I not been paralysed with fear, I would have uttered the most unmanly scream my parched throat could muster. Yet alas, I watched this grotesque theatrical show, the dirty ground my seat; the gnarled, rough wood my cushion; and the cold, dead lamp my popcorn bowl. I watched helplessly, as spineless as denizens who see their country destroyed but who are powerless to interfere.

The wind drowned out whatever horrible spells the poltergeists uttered. They stood in a circle whose centre was occupied by a small child tied to the central wooden pillar in the henge. The child, be it a he or a she (for it was indiscernible in the dark), was naked, save for a rag around its waist. It cried in vulnerability as the spectres chanted maniacally around it. Finally, one of the figures, whose stature and build identified him as a male, strode forward and pulled a hood over his face. I caught a fleeting flash of metal, and gasped in horror as realization struck me. It was a sacrificial knife, rough at the edges and blunt. The hooded figure stood in front of the child. Crying loudly, he slit the youngster's throat in one quick slash, and filled a small wooden bowl with the gushing fountain of blood. The child quivered as its soul bled away, and it soon ceased to move.

The eidolons then added oil to the blood and lit the ghastly concoction ablaze. They left it at the feet of the child, where the conflagration quickly engulfed its skin in flames. The figures stood motionless around, watching with interest, as if the scene before them was not the result of their actions. The sky rumbled loudly, as though some metaphysical deity was appeased by the massacre. The figures prayed, and so did I.

O Merciful Lord, I said, *protect me in my hour of need. Bless me with a painless death whose swiftness is none other than a mercy from You. Let me die 'fore my death is pronounced with that kni—* And with these ravings in mind, I found myself unconscious, adrift and free. I embraced that sleep, for I thought that it was the lethargy of death.

The next day, I awoke to find myself in the same awkward position on the ground. My back felt as stiff as the tree I slept against. The sun was shining high in the sky, and its warmth gave me energy to move. Some life returned to my hands and feet, no doubt due to the sun's heat. Standing up, I waited for my sleepy thighs to regain balance before standing. The wind, formerly a maelstrom, had become a gentle breeze. I limped and hobbled all the way to my car. O my beloved car! Settling comfortably into the soft leather seat I turned on the heating system and drove off. With one last glance, I looked onto the henge—that monstrous origin of all that as barbarous—and sped off down the one-way lane.

The following day, emboldened by companionship, I told my colleagues that they ought to accompany me to Woodhenge for a visit. *Why* I did not answer, but told them to escort me nevertheless. Entering the malicious place again, I did one thing only. I strode purposefully to the centre of the henge, where that accursed mound once stood, with my associates tailing me. The shovel was still where I had left it on the fifteenth, its blade halfway buried in the ground. I hauled dirt until I unearthed the skull beneath. Groaning in disgust, my comrades averted their eyes. In that moment, with my friends' attention scattered, I swear in God's name thrice that the skull *somehow* turned itself to my direction and *grinned*.

We left everything as it was and left hastily. Whatever occurred on the fifteenth of December, the night of the Winter solstice, I don't know; and I don't *want* to know. However, I know that I won't *ever again* tread a foot in the accursed woods of Woodhenge.

Noises at Higham Hill

13 October

Dear Truman,

I have just moved into Higham Hill. And, O God, I am already hell-bent on deserting that loathsome house by the lake. Doubtless it is that you are pondering the reasons I left the metropolis and chose to live in this godforsaken land. Rest assured, I was—and still am (mostly)—sane. It all started with a newspaper.

A couple of weeks ago I chanced upon an advertisement for a house called Higham Hill situated on an isolated piece of land by the lake. Piqued with interest, I journeyed through the countryside until I reached Higham. And what a disappointment it was! Aye, aye, the land was vast and vacant, surrounded with a forest belt which fully isolated the house from its neighbours. However, lichen and moss outgrew everything there, climbing on walls, gnawing on everything adjacent to it. Unshaven grass grew everywhere, its dank, soggy roots giving off a terrible, nauseating stench.

And that was the outdoors *only*. The landlord took it upon himself to show me around the house. It was dismal and dreary. The wallpaper was tattered in numerous patches, leaving behind gaping open holes which I guess would have looked similar to Satan's maw. The furniture was antiquated, looking fragile and brittle in the dim light. The rooms were many, but each one was smaller than a woman's cabinet. And thus I was dissatisfied, and wholly bent on leaving the dilapidated, repulsive house to its owner.

However, *here* came the dilemma. Just as I was giving my thanks to the landlord, he caught my wrist tightly and, with sweat dripping down his neck, *begged* me to buy the house! I apologised considerably, saying that I was low on money and could not possibly afford the house. He was not deterred, and whispered in my ear a price too good to be true, a price which I feel obliged to call *wallet-friendly*. I will not mention the price in figures, as you know that I am touchy about money, but suffice it is to say that I agreed to the offer almost instantly.

In that particular moment, I fancied that I heard shrill singing emanating from the house. When I inquired about that, the landlord, swiping his temple with a handkerchief, said, "Ooh, pardon! I am sure it's that lousy maid, singing again with her piercing voice! Aye, aye, she does shatter half the windows in this house with that voice of hers!" Although I did not recall seeing any maids scurrying about the house, I digested this statement without scrutiny.

A week or so after the deal was sealed, with the transaction between the landlord and I fully settled to the mutual satisfaction of both parties, I moved into Higham Hill. All went smoothly. I brought with me my two faithful servants to look after the house. After the movers had left, I was more than aware of how foreboding and ominous the house actually was. An omnipresent evil seemed to be lurking within the far shadows.

Nothing of importance occurred in the last couple of weeks so as to be included in this letter. Last night, however, unsettlement began. I was reclining on a soft pillow, forcing myself to sleep, when I heard them—rhythmic knocks. I woke frightfully, and gazing around, could not find the source of this untimely disturbance—that is, until I realised the raps were coming from *behind* the wall.

I threw the bedcovers over my head, attempting to ignore the knocks. But no matter, they kept hammering into my ears, refusing to abate. Groaning in irritation, I shifted positions, all in the attempt to drown out the merciless noise, yet to no avail. *Knock, knock, and … knock.*

Just as I was approaching the brink of madness, a scream ripped apart the quiet fabric of the night. The scream was so loud, in fact, that I was sure half the neighbourhood heard it. And with the scream's fading echoes, the knocks also faded into oblivion. I began shivering, and not a wink of sleep crossed my face before the break of dawn.

The following day, I asked the servants if they had heard any disruptive sounds during the night. They replied with the negative, testifying that nothing broke their continuous snoring. Whether the racket I heard was a production of my sickly imagination or not, I do not know, but I know that Higham Hill has sordid secrets hidden beneath its decaying walls—secrets I have yet to discover.

Yours in light and dark,
Jacob Burnaby

****

20 October
Dear Truman,

I am terribly inclined to call my new house, Higham Hill, *Higham Hell*. My nerves are more than just shaken, and as of late I have perceived knocks and other abrupt noises. My work colleagues have nicknamed me Jumpy Jacob. I do agree with them that I am now always on edge. My toiling servants have become increasingly uneasy, muttering superstitions whenever I am out of earshot. "Only a Satanic fool dwells in such a Satanic dwelling", I heard one say.

Well, you see, the knocks have become well-nigh a nocturnal ritual, commencing at midnight and ending every night with that bloodcurdling scream. I have not identified the source of these horrifying howls. (I fear they emanate from the nether depths of hell.) But I have settled on one fact: these noises are the product of a terrible entity haunting the house of Higham Hill, which I have settled on naming 'the poltergeist'. By what ominous circumstances this poltergeist came to haunt Higham Hill I know not, but I am sure that soon enough a final confrontation will occur between us, the victor of which will dwell in Higham.

As I promised that I'd keep you up-to-date on any new developments in concern with Higham, I have decided to send you this letter as hastily as possible. You see, my notion that an inevitable confrontation is brewing has been gleaned from a strange occurrence which happened to me yesterday.

It was about an hour before midnight. I was reading a book, with the lamplight throwing feeble, dancing shadows across the dark corners of my bedroom. My eyelids were drooping, and my eyes were aching, yet I felt an insomnious form of sleeplessness, doubtlessly induced from my fears of the poltergeist. Closing the book, I turned off the lamp and yawned helplessly. I then slid into the soft, protective sheets of my bed, covered myself with the duvet, and slept.

Just as I was on the brink of sleep, a melodious singing erupted into the night. It was poignant and heart-wrenching, evoking a sense of regret. Jerking awake, I looked around me, expecting to find the poltergeist. However, as is usual, the sounds were coming from the wall. They bore an identical resemblance to the shrill singing I heard upon my first visit of the house. And as far as my rusty mind could recollect, the song went like this:

> O ye of little faith,
> 'fraid are ye of a wraith?
> A man, ho ho, he saith.
> Flee if thee wishes no scathe.

The rest was incomprehensible gibberish. The singing slowly mutated into that frightful scream, awakening everyone within the household ... then there was silence. I had been knocked unconscious. The servants, who came rushing to my bedroom, found me in a maddened state, tearing at the blanket whilst grovelling on the floor of my bedroom. Later on, they told me that I had been drooling uncontrollably, all the whilst murmuring, "Flee if thee wishes no scathe".

The following day, I drove an hour to the nearest town to meet with a physician. He prescribed an extensive list of antidepressants and sleeping drugs, including benzodiazepine, which just tells how severe my psychological state of mind actually was. I was bent on sharing my inner fears with the physician, but sensing his scientifically-oriented mind, I knew that he would only laugh at me.

Dear friend, I write to you in a time of need. If for any reason you find me knocking at your doors seeking refuge, please refuse me not. I am frightened of Higham Hill and believe that there is a danger brewing in the dark clouds of the future.

Yours unto the end,
Jacob Burnaby

23 October

Dear Truman,

Well, well, hereby I announce the utter annihilation of my morale. Truman, I am in quite the fix indeed. Up until recently, this poltergeist used three tactics to scare me out of my wits: knocks, screams, and singing. Now the poltergeist has begun destroying furniture and household items. More than once, the night passed silently, that is until I heard a scraping sound ululating deep within the house. I then remained shaken and far too afraid to take action. At morning, I would descend forlornly down the creaky stairs to find another piece of furniture—be it a chair or cabinet—mutilated beyond recognition, scarred with claw-like marks.

Oh, yes! I almost forgot to tell you—the servants have deserted me. They left two days ago, telling me they could not possibly withstand the devilry of this house. I must agree. There is an aura of malice surrounding the place, as if exuding some form of twisted enchantment. Last night was the final stroke that assured me of the existence of this poltergeist.

The wind was roaring, with savage storms hammering on through the night. I was huddling alone in the house, waiting for a truce between the fighting gods of the sky. Heavy torrents of rain pounded the roof, and I am sure that, had I survived the night without fleeing from Higham Hill, I would have seen the house scoured for the first time of lichen and moss.

I was sitting in my office, rifling through papers of no relevance to you. The yellow lamplight was so feeble that I had to hunch over and squint in order to read. Then suddenly—*pzzt!*—the power went out. It took me a couple of seconds to realize that the electricity was dead. Fazed, I stumbled blindly down the stairs to the cupboard underneath them. I had bought a bunch of candles for times like these, and cursing wildly, fumbled about to locate them. After finally igniting one, I took it with me upstairs to my bedroom. I placed it beside me, keeping it close for both warmth and light.

Outside, the ferocious beast that was the wind became even fiercer. Unholy echoes reverberated across the night. My heart began pumping blood faster, as sweat dripped from my forehead. If only you knew how frightened I was, Truman! And for apparently no viable reason, the candlelight winked out suddenly. You would wonder why I didn't light up the candle again, but you should know that just as I was going to fetch the matchsticks, the horrendous knocks came back again from behind the wall!

I was paralysed. The knocks became almost like the prelude to an orchestral masterpiece, beginning with knocks, flaring into screams, and mercifully ending in the fading echoes of the revolting singing of that poltergeist. Just like a dumb-witted ostrich, I buried my face in a pillow, whilst the singing continued:

> O' ye of little faith,
> 'fraid are ye of a wraith?
> A man, ho ho, he saith.
> Flee if thee wishes no scathe.

I lifted my head off the pillow. Total darkness greeted me. The maddening singing has stopped. However, a pair of red orbs—a pair of blood-red orbs—hovered a couple of metres from me. I felt blood drain from my face and my throat contract as I realized that these hovering orbs were actually eyes. The poltergeist then came into light, from where I couldn't discern. It had a faceless, featureless head, with thick curls of hair tumbling onto its shoulders. It had a normal human body—that is, except for its arms, which were clawed with elongated talons, dripping with blood.

The monster took a step toward me. Its featureless head was bowed down, as if from timidity. To this day, I don't know what actually possessed my bowels so to withstand such terror without loosing themselves. The poltergeist advanced silently, its body hovering nearer and nearer toward me. With a loud, a sort of delirium assaulted me. The spell which held me motionless was broken, and I found myself sprinting crazily through the halls of Higham Hill.

Nothing beyond that, I am quite ashamed to confess, do I remember, for my mind was so much fazed that I did not register anything that I passed by. I woke next day sprawled beside a farm a couple of miles away from Higham Hill. I was soiled head to toe in mud. Thank goodness that I had my wallet! The owner of the farm took it upon himself to take me in. He gave me a change of clothes, and drove me up the way station in order to take a train to the metropolis.

I am actually writing this letter in the station as I await my train. My dear friend, even at this moment, with the bustling crowds surrounding me, I am still shivering from my frightful experience at Higham Hill. Whether the phantom that haunts that hellish house is the first inhabitant of Higham *Hell* I don't know. Some mysteries are better left undisturbed. I am sure that the poltergeist is now atop Higham Hill, laughing hysterically at the weakness of humans. "Another victory! Now who's the next on the list?" it would be saying with its faceless head.

The train's whistling. Truman, I am coming!

Yours truly in heaven and *hill*,
Jacob Burnaby